FÜN學美國各學科

Preschool 閱讀課本 二版

AMERiCAN
SCHOOL
TEXTBOOK

Reading Key

5

Preschool
初學單字篇

作者 ◎ Michael A. Putlack &
e-Creative Contents

譯者 ◎ 歐寶妮

U0033682

Authors

Michael A. Putlack

Michael A. Putlack graduated from Tufts University in Medford, Massachusetts, USA, where he got his B.A. in History and English and his M.A. in History. He has written a number of books for children, teenagers, and adults.

e-Creative Contents

A creative group that develops English contents and products for ESL and EFL students.

The Best Preparation for Building Basic Vocabulary and Grammar

The Reading Key — Preschool series is designed to help children understand basic words and grammar to learn English. This series also helps children develop their reading skills in a fun and easy way.

Features

- Learning high-frequency words that appear in all kinds of reading material
- Building basic grammar and reading comprehension skills to learn English
- Various activities including reading and writing practice
- A wide variety of topics that cover American school subjects
- Full-color photographs and illustrations

The Reading Key series has five levels.

- Reading Key **Preschool 1–6**
  a six-book series designed for preschoolers and kindergarteners

- Reading Key **Basic 1–4**
  a four-book series designed for kindergarteners and beginners

- Reading Key **Volume 1–3**
  a three-book series designed for beginner to intermediate learners

- Reading Key **Volume 4–6**
  a three-book series designed for intermediate to high-intermediate learners

- Reading Key **Volume 7–9**
  a three-book series designed for high-intermediate learners

Table of Contents | Preschool 5
My First Words

Components Workbook for Daily Review • Answers and Translations

Syllabus | Preschool 5
My First Words

Subject	Unit	Grammar	Vocabulary
Basic Words Kids Need to Know **Common Nouns and Adjectives**	**Unit 1** **Colors ❶**	• **Adjectives for colors** • **Adjectives that describe nouns**	• red, yellow, blue, green • hen, chick, bird, tree • a red car/a yellow bus/a blue bicycle/ a green taxi
	Unit 2 **Colors ❷**	• **Adjectives for colors** • **Adjectives that describe nouns**	• orange, brown, black, white, black and white • cat, dog, bear, penguin • an orange carrot/a brown bear/ a black cat/a white dog/a black and white penguin
	Unit 3 **Shapes ❶**	• **Adjectives & nouns for shapes** • **Adjectives that describe nouns** • **Singular and plural nouns**	• circle, square, triangle, rectangle • ball, chocolate, pyramid, board • two circles/two triangles/two squares/ two rectangles
	Unit 4 **Shapes ❷**	• **Adjectives & nouns for shapes** • **Adjectives that describe nouns**	• diamond, star, oval, heart • road sign, cookie, egg, gift box • a yellow diamond/a blue star/ a brown oval/a red heart • diamond shape/oval shape/heart shape/ star shape
	Unit 5 **My Family**	• **Common nouns for family** • **Present continuous (Be + V-ing)**	• grandmother, grandfather, mother, father, sister, brother • younger sister/older brother • watching TV/cooking/reading a book/ singing a song
	Unit 6 **At School**	• **Common nouns for school** • **Present continuous (Be + V-ing)** • **Prepositions of location**	• teacher, student • classroom, playground, library, cafeteria • reading/writing/painting/playing • in the library/in the classroom/ in the cafeteria/on the playground/ on the board
	Unit 7 **After School ❶**	• **Common nouns for activities** • **Present continuous (Be + V-ing)**	• cycling, jogging, roller-skating, swimming • ice skating, skiing, snowboarding, sledding • playing soccer/playing baseball/ playing basketball/playing volleyball
	Unit 8 **After School ❷**	• **Common nouns for activities** • **Present simple**	• art class, English class, math class, piano class • dance class, soccer practice, taekwondo class, swimming class • go to/goes to

Colors ①

Key Words Read the words.

red

yellow

blue

green

hen

chick

bird

tree

Match Up

Match the words with the pictures.

red

blue

yellow

green

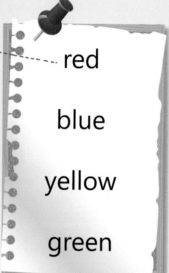

hen

chick

bird

tree

What Color?

Put a check under the correct picture.

a car

a bus

a bicycle

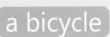

a taxi

☑

a red car

a yellow bus

a blue bicycle

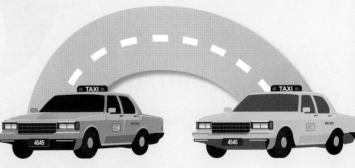

a green taxi

What Is It?

Circle the correct word for each sentence.

It is a (hen , chick).

It is a (hen , chick).

It is a (bird , tree).

It is a (bird , tree).

What Color Is It?

Circle the correct word for each sentence.

It is red.
It is a (red, **yellow**) hen.

It is yellow.
It is a (**yellow, blue**) chick.

It is blue.
It is a (**yellow, blue**) bird.

It is green.
It is a (**green, red**) tree.

11

I Can Read

Read the story.
Draw Lines to the right pictures.

What Am I?

I am big.
I am red.
What am I?

I am little.
I am yellow.
What am I?

Colors 2

 Key Words Read the words.

orange

brown

black

white

black and white

cat

dog

bear

penguin

Match Up

Match the words with the pictures.

orange ----------

brown

black

white

black and white

What Color?

Put a check under the correct picture.

a carrot a bear a cat a dog a penguin

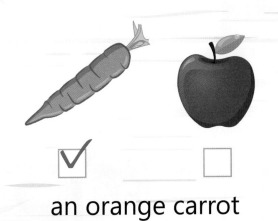

☑ ☐

an orange carrot

☐ ☐

a brown bear

☐ ☐

a black cat

☐ ☐

a white dog

☐ ☐

a black and white penguin

What Is It?

Circle the correct word for each sentence.

It is a (**cat**, **dog**).

It is a (**cat**, **dog**).

It is a (**bear**, **bird**).

It is a (**penguin**, **bear**).

It is a (**carrot**, **cat**).

What Color Is It?

Circle the correct word for each sentence.

It is white.
It is a (white, black) cat.

It is black.
It is a (white, black) dog.

It is brown.
It is a (brown, white) bear.

It is black and white.
It is a (black and white, black and brown) penguin.

It is orange.
It is an (orange, yellow) carrot.

I Can Read

Read the story.
<u>Draw Lines</u> to the right pictures.

What Am I?

I am big.
I am brown.
What am I?

I am little.
I am white.
What am I?

I am big.
I am black and white.
What am I?

I am little.
I am black.
What am I?

Shapes ①

 Key Words Read the words.

circle

square

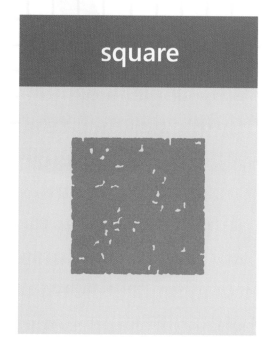

triangle

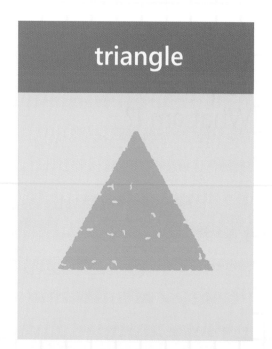

rectangle

ball

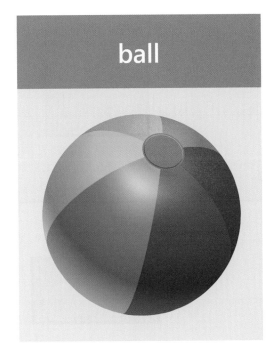

chocolate

pyramid

board

Match Up

Match the words with the pictures.

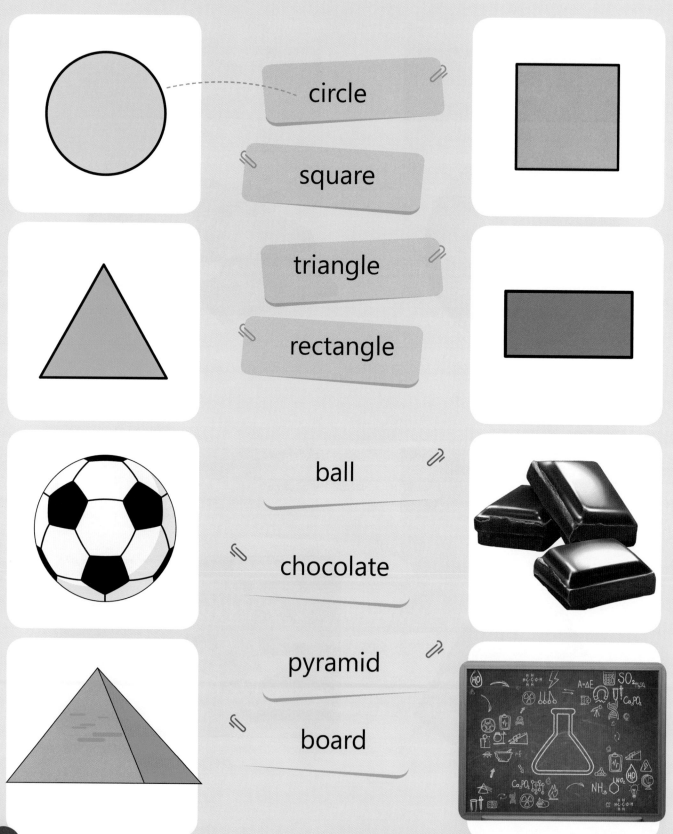

circle

square

triangle

rectangle

ball

chocolate

pyramid

board

What Shape Is It?

(Circle) the words **in blue**.

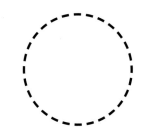

It is a circle.

It is a red circle.

It is a square.

It is a blue square.

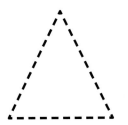

It is a triangle.

It is a yellow triangle.

It is a rectangle.

It is a green rectangle.

Circle the words **in blue**.

There is a circle.

There are two circles.

There is a triangle.

There are two triangles.

There is a square.

There are two squares.

There is a rectangle.

There are two rectangles.

 **I See**

Circle the correct word for each sentence.

I see a red ball.
It is a (**circle** , **square**).

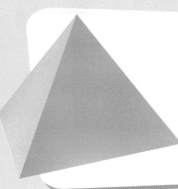

I see a yellow pyramid.
It is a (**triangle** , **rectangle**).

I see a brown chocolate.
It is a (**square** , **circle**).

I see a green board.
It is a (**rectangle** , **square**).

I Can Read

Read the story.

(Circle) the correct words.

What Do You See?

What do you see?
I see two blue (**squares** , **rectangles**).

What do you see?
I see two red (**circles** , **triangles**).

What do you see?
I see one yellow (**triangle, circle**).

What do you see?
I see two green (**rectangles, squares**).

Shapes ②

 Key Words Read the words.

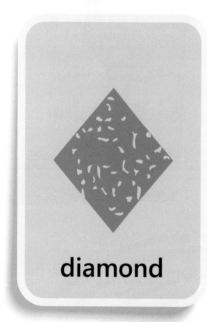

diamond

star

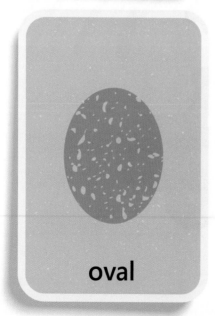

oval

heart

road sign

cookie

egg

gift box

Match Up

Match the words with the pictures.

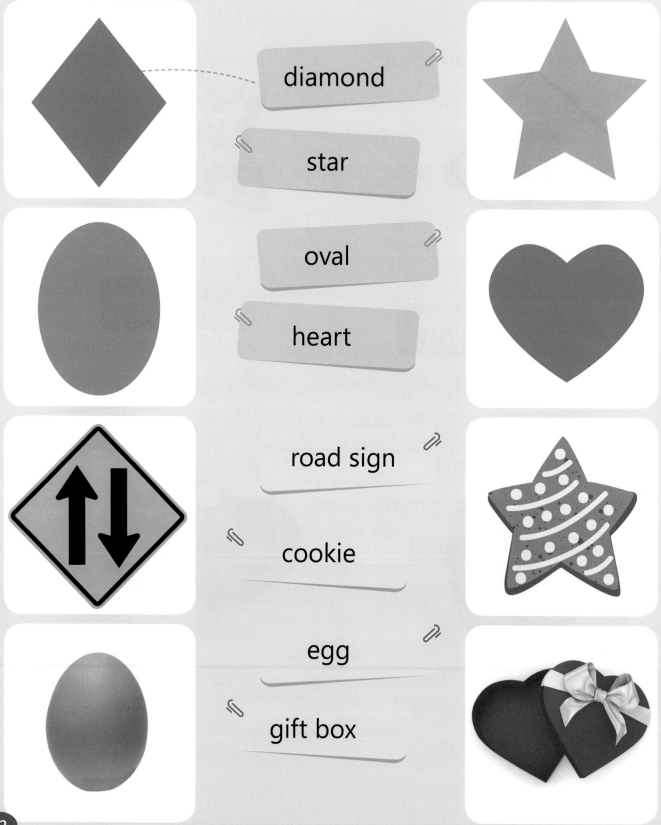

diamond

star

oval

heart

road sign

cookie

egg

gift box

What Shape Is It?

(Circle) the words **in blue**.

It is a diamond.

It is a yellow diamond.

It is a star.

It is a blue star.

It is an oval.

It is a brown oval.

It is a heart.

It is a red heart.

Is It a Star?

Circle the words **in blue**.

Is it a star?

Yes, it is.

Is it a heart?

Yes, it is.

Is it a rectangle?

No, it isn't.
It is a diamond.

Is it a circle?

No, it isn't.
It is an oval.

What Is It?

Circle the correct word for each sentence.

It is a road sign.

It is a (**diamond**, **heart**) shape.

It is an egg.

It is an (**oval**, **circle**) shape.

It is a gift box.

It is a (**heart**, **oval**) shape.

It is a cookie.

It is a (**star**, **heart**) shape.

I Can Read

Read the story.
Circle the words **in blue**.

> ## What Can You See?

I can see many stars.
They are blue and white.

I can see many hearts.
They are red.

I can see many diamonds.
They are white.

I can see many eggs.
They are oval shapes.

Review Test 1

| square | circle | rectangle | triangle | brown | orange | black and white |

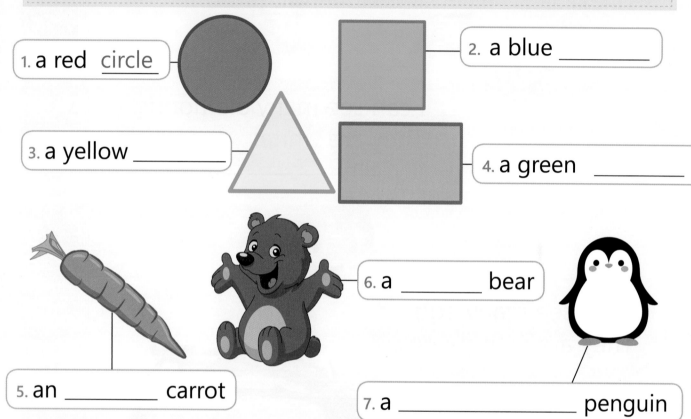

1. a red _circle_

2. a blue _____

3. a yellow _____

4. a green _____

5. an _____ carrot

6. a _____ bear

7. a _____ penguin

B Circle the correct answer for each sentence.

1. I see a red (**hen**, **chick**).

2. I see a yellow (**pyramid, chocolate**).

3. I see a green (**ball, board**).

4. I see an (**oval, diamond**) egg.

Circle the correct answer for each sentence.

1. Is it a circle?
   No, it isn't. It is an (**oval**, **star**).

2. Is it a rectangle?
   No, it isn't. It is a (**circle, triangle**).

3. Is it a heart shape?
   No, it isn't. It is a (**diamond, star**) shape.

4. Is it a diamond shape?
   No, it isn't. It is a (**heart, oval**) shape.

D **Match the sentences with the pictures.**

1. It is a chick.
   It is a yellow chick.

2. It is a chocolate.
   It is a brown chocolate.

3. It is a gift box.
   It is a heart shape.

4. It is a road sign.
   It is a diamond shape.

My Family

Key Words Read the words.

grandmother

grandma

grandfather

grandpa

mother

mom

father

dad

sister

older brother

brother

younger sister

Match Up

Match the words with the pictures.

mother   father   brother   grandfather

sister   grandmother

watch TV

cook

read a book

sing a song

Who Is This?

Circle the correct word for each sentence.

This is my (**mother**, father).

This is my (**mother**, **father**).

This is my (**sister**, **brother**).

This is my (**sister**, **brother**).

This is my (**grandmother**, **grandfather**).

This is my (**grandmother**, **grandfather**).

Is This Your Sister?

Circle the words **Yes** and **is**.

Underline the words **No** and **isn't**.

Is this your sister?

Yes, it is.

She is my younger sister.

Is this your brother?

Yes, it is.

He is my older brother.

Is this your father?

No, it isn't.

He is my grandfather.

Is this your mother?

No, it isn't.

She is my grandmother.

What Is She Doing?

Circle the words with **-ing**.

My mom is cooking.

My dad is watching TV.

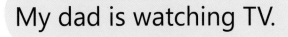

My sister is reading a book.

My brother is singing a song.

My grandpa is reading a newspaper.

I Can Read

Read the story. Circle the words **in blue**.

What is Dad doing?

He is reading a newspaper.

What is Mom doing?

She is cooking.

What is my sister doing?

She is singing a song.

What is my grandpa doing?

He is watching TV.

At School

 Key Words Read the words.

teacher

classroom

student

playground

library

cafeteria

reading

writing

painting

playing

Match Up

Match the words with the pictures.

teacher

student

classroom

playground

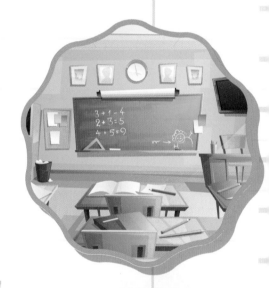

library

cafeteria

What Is He Doing?

Circle the correct word for each sentence.

The boy is (**reading** , **writing**).

The girl is (**playing** , **painting**).

The teacher is (**reading** , **writing**).

Ben is (**playing** , **painting**).

Ann is (**eating** , **eat**) lunch.

51

Is She Doing?

Circle the words **Yes** and **is**.

Underline the words **No** and **isn't**.

 Is the girl reading a book?

 Yes, she is.

Is the boy playing?

Yes, he is.

 Is the teacher singing?

 No, she isn't. She is writing.

Is the student writing?

No, he isn't. He is painting.

Where Is She?

Circle the correct word for each sentence.

The girl is reading in the (**library**, **playground**).

The boy is playing on the (**library**, **playground**).

Ben is painting in the (**classroom**, **cafeteria**).

Ann is eating lunch in the (**classroom**, **cafeteria**).

The teacher is writing on the (**board**, **table**).

I Can Read

Read the story. Circle the words **in blue**.

This is Jane.
She is painting in the classroom.

This is Ben.
He is reading a book in the library.

This is Mike.
He is playing on the playground.

This is Ann.
She is writing on the board.

After school ①

37 Key Words Read the words.

cycling

jogging

roller-skating

swimming

ice skating

skiing

snowboarding

sledding

playing soccer

playing baseball

playing basketball

playing volleyball

Match Up

Match the words with the pictures.

cycling

jogging

roller-skating

swimming

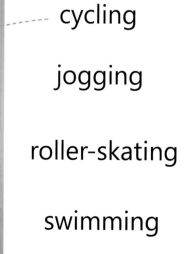

ice skating

skiing

snowboarding

sledding

What Are They Doing?

Circle the correct word for each sentence.

They are (**jogging**, **cycling**).

They are (**roller-skating**, **ice skating**).

They are (**cycling**, **sledding**).

They are (**swimming**, **skiing**).

Are They Doing?

Circle the words **Yes** and **are**.

Underline the words **No** and **aren't**.

Are they ice skating?

Yes, they are.

Are they skiing?

Yes, they are.

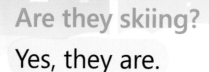

Are they snowboarding?

No, they aren't.
They're sledding.

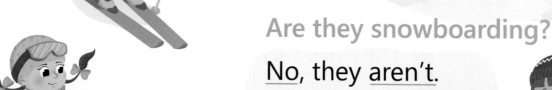

Are they sledding?

No, they aren't. They're snowboarding.

Are You Doing?

Underline the words **in blue**.

Are you playing soccer?

Yes, I am.

Are you playing baseball?

Yes, I am.

Are you playing volleyball?

No, I'm not.
I'm playing basketball.

Are you playing basketball?

No, I'm not.
I'm playing volleyball.

I Can Read

Read the story. Underline the words **in blue**.

What Are They Doing?

The boy is <u>snowboarding</u>.

The girls are skiing.

The boys are sledding.

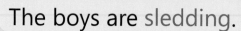

The boy is jogging in the park.

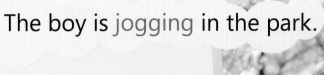

The girl is roller-skating in the park.

The boys are playing baseball in the park.

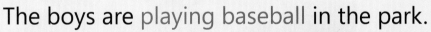

8 After school 2

 Key Words Read the words.

art class

English class

math class

piano class

dance class

soccer practice

taekwondo class

swimming class

Match Up

Match the words with the pictures.

art class

English class

math class

piano class

dance class

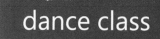

soccer practice

taekwondo class

swimming class

I Go to

Circle the words **in blue**.

I go to English class.

I go to math class.

I go to piano class.

I go to art class.

I go to dance class.

He Goes to

Circle the words **in blue**.

He goes to soccer practice.

She goes to swimming class.

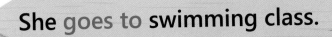

He goes to taekwondo class.

Jane goes to dance class.

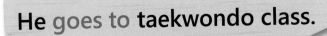

Ben goes to piano class.

What Do You Do?

Circle the correct word for each sentence.

What do you do after school?

I go to (**math**, **English**) class.

What do you do after school?

I go to (**art**, **piano**) class.

What do you do after school?

I go to (**art**, **piano**) class.

What do you do after school?

I go to (**dance**, **swimming**) class.

I Can Read

Read the story. Draw lines to the right pictures.

What Does He Do?

What does she do after school **?**

What does he do after school **?**

She goes to swimming class.

He goes to soccer practice.

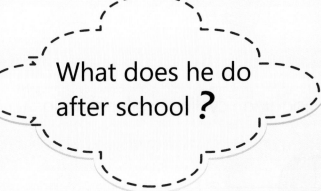

What does he do
after school **?**

He goes to taekwondo class.

What does she
do after school **?**

She goes to dance class.

Review Test 2

A Choose and write.

classroom library playground cafeteria jogging cycling roller-skating

1. classroom

2.

3.

4.

5.

6.

7.

B Circle the correct answer for each sentence.

1. My dad is (**watching TV**, cooking).

2. My grandpa is reading a (**book, newspaper**).

3. The boy is playing on the (**library, playground**).

4. The teacher is (**painting, writing**) on the board.

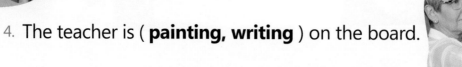

72

72

Circle the correct answer for each sentence.

1. Are they snowboarding?
No, they aren't. They're (**sledding**, **ice skating**).

2. Are they playing soccer?
No, they aren't. They're playing (**basketball**, **volleyball**).

3. Is the girl skiing?
No, she isn't. She is (**snowboarding**, **sledding**).

4. Is the boy jogging?
No, he isn't. He is (**roller-skating**, **ice skating**).

 Match the sentences with the pictures.

1. The boy goes to soccer practice. •

2. The girl goes to swimming class. •

3. Ben goes to taekwondo class. •

4. Jane goes to art class.

Word List

Colors ❶
顏色 ❶

1	**red**	紅色；紅色的
2	**yellow**	黃色；黃色的
3	**blue**	藍色；藍色的
4	**green**	綠色；綠色的
5	**hen**	母雞
6	**chick**	小雞
7	**bird**	鳥
8	**tree**	樹
9	**a car**	一輛汽車
10	**a bus**	一台公車
11	**a bicycle**	一台腳踏車
12	**a taxi**	一輛計程車
13	**a red car**	一輛紅色的汽車
14	**a yellow bus**	一輛黃色的公車
15	**a blue bicycle**	一台藍色的腳踏車
16	**a green taxi**	一台綠色的計程車
17	**What is it?**	它是什麼？
18	**It is . . .**	它是……
19	**What color is it?**	它是什麼顏色？
20	**What am I?**	我是什麼？
21	**I am big.**	我很大。
22	**I am little.**	我很小。

Colors ❷
顏色 ❷

1	**orange**	橘黃色；橘黃色的
2	**brown**	棕色；棕色的
3	**black**	黑色；黑色的
4	**white**	白色；白色的
5	**black and white**	黑白相間；黑白相間的
6	**cat**	貓
7	**dog**	狗
8	**bear**	熊
9	**penguin**	企鵝
10	**a carrot**	一根胡蘿蔔

11	**a bear**	一隻熊
12	**a cat**	一隻貓
13	**a dog**	一隻狗
14	**a penguin**	一隻企鵝
15	**an orange carrot**	一根橘黃色的胡蘿蔔
16	**a brown bear**	一隻棕色的熊
17	**a black cat**	一隻黑色的貓
18	**a white dog**	一隻白色的狗
19	**a black and white penguin**	一隻黑白相間的企鵝

Unit 3

Shapes ❶
形狀 ❶

1	**circle**	圓形
2	**square**	正方形
3	**triangle**	三角形
4	**rectangle**	長方形
5	**ball**	球
6	**chocolate**	巧克力
7	**pyramid**	金字塔；三角錐
8	**board**	板子
9	**What shape is it?**	它是什麼形狀？
10	**a red circle**	一個紅色的圓形
11	**a blue square**	一個藍色的正方形
12	**a yellow triangle**	一個黃色的三角形

13	**a green rectangle**	一個綠色的長方形
14	**a circle**	一個圓形
15	**two circles**	兩個圓形
16	**a triangle**	一個三角形
17	**two triangles**	兩個三角形
18	**a square**	一個正方形
19	**two squares**	兩個正方形
20	**a rectangle**	一個長方形
21	**two rectangles**	兩個長方形
22	**I see . . .**	我看到……
23	**I see a red ball.**	我看到一顆紅色的球。
24	**What do you see?**	你看到了什麼？

Unit 4

Shapes ❷
形狀 ❷

1	**diamond**	菱形；菱形的
2	**star**	星形；星形的
3	**oval**	橢圓形；橢圓形的
4	**heart**	心形；心形的
5	**road sign**	道路標示
6	**cookie**	餅乾
7	**egg**	蛋
8	**gift box**	禮物盒
9	**a yellow diamond**	一個黃色的菱形
10	**a blue star**	一個藍色的星形
11	**a brown oval**	一個棕色的橢圓形

12 **a red heart** 一個紅色的心形

13 Ⓐ**Is it a star?** 它是星形嗎？

Ⓑ**Yes, it is.** 對，它是。

Ⓑ**No, it isn't.** 不，它不是。

14 **What is it?** 這是什麼？

15 **a diamond shape** 一個菱形的形狀

16 **an oval shape** 一個橢圓形的形狀

17 **a heart shape** 一個心形的形狀

18 **a star shape** 一個星形的形狀

19 **What can you see?** 你可以看到什麼？

Unit 5

My Family
我的家人

1 **grandmother (= grandma)**
奶奶；外婆；祖母

2 **grandfather (= grandpa)**
爺爺；外公；祖父

3 **mother (= mom)**
母親；媽媽

4 **father (= dad)** 父親；爸爸

5 **sister** 姊妹

6 **brother** 兄弟

7 **younger sister** 妹妹

8 **older brother** 哥哥

9 **watch TV** 看電視

10 **cook** 做菜

11 **read a book** 閱讀書籍

12 **sing a song** 唱歌

13 **Who is this?** 這是誰？

14 **This is . . .** 這是……

15 Ⓐ**Is this your sister?**
這是你的姊妹嗎？

Ⓑ**Yes, it is.** 是的，她是。

Ⓑ**No, it isn't.** 不，她不是。

16 **What is she doing?**
她正在做什麼？

17 **My mom is cooking.**
我媽正在做菜。

18 **My dad is watching TV.**
我爸正在看電視。

19 **My sister is reading a book.**
我的姐姐正在閱讀書籍。

20 **My brother is singing a song.**
我的弟弟正在唱歌。

21 **My grandpa is reading a newspaper.**
我的爺爺正在看報紙。

Unit 6

At School
在學校

1 **teacher** 老師

2 **student** 學生

3 **classroom** 教室

4 **playground** 操場；運動場；遊樂場

5 **library** 圖書館

6 **cafeteria** 自助餐館

7 **reading**　　　　閱讀

8 **writing**　　　　寫字；寫作

9 **painting**　　　　畫畫

10 **playing**　　　　玩；演奏

11 **What is he doing?**
他正在做什麼？

12 **The boy is reading.**
那個男孩正在閱讀。

13 **The girl is playing.**
那個女孩正在玩。

14 **The teacher is writing.**
那位老師正在寫字。

15 **Ben is painting.**
班正在畫畫。

16 **Ann is eating lunch.**
安正在吃午餐。

17 Ⓐ**Is the girl reading a book?**
那個女孩正在閱讀書籍嗎？

　 Ⓑ**Yes, she is.**　　對，她正在閱讀書籍。

　 Ⓑ**No, she isn't.**
不，她沒有在閱讀書籍。

18 **Where is she?**　她在哪裡？

19 **in the library**　　在圖書館裡

20 **on the playground**　在操場上

21 **in the classroom**　　在教室裡

22 **in the cafeteria**　　在自助餐館

23 **on the board**　　　在板子上

After School ❶
放學後 ❶

1 **cycling**　　　　騎腳踏車

2 **jogging**　　　　慢跑

3 **roller-skating**　輪式溜冰；溜直排輪

4 **swimming**　　　游泳

5 **ice skating**　　溜冰

6 **skiing**　　　　滑雪

7 **snowboarding**　單板滑雪

8 **sledding**　　　乘雪橇

9 **playing soccer** 踢足球

10 **playing baseball**　打棒球

11 **playing basketball**　打籃球

12 **playing volleyball**　打排球

13 **What are they doing?**
他們正在做什麼？

14 **They are jogging.**
他們正在慢跑。

15 **They are roller-skating.**
他們正在溜直排輪。

16 **They are cycling.**
他們正在騎腳踏車。

17 **They are swimming.**
他們正在游泳。

18 Ⓐ**Are they ice skating?**
他們正在溜冰嗎？

　 Ⓑ**Yes, they are.**
對，他們在溜冰。

B No, they aren't.
不，他們沒有在溜冰。

19 **A** Are you playing soccer?
你正在踢足球嗎？

B Yes, I am.
對，我正在踢足球。

B No, I'm not.
不，我沒有在踢足球。

Unit 8

After School 2
放學後 2

1 **art class** 美術課

2 **English class** 英文課

3 **math class** 數學課

4 **piano class** 鋼琴課

5 **dance class** 舞蹈課

6 **soccer practice** 足球練習

7 **taekwondo class** 跆拳道課

8 **swimming class** 游泳課

9 **I go to** 我去

10 **I go to English class.**
我去上英文課。

11 **I go to math class.**
我去上數學課。

12 **I go to piano class.**
我去上鋼琴課。

13 **I go to art class.**
我去上美術課。

14 **I go to dance class.**
我去上舞蹈課。

15 **He goes to** 他去

16 **He goes to soccer practice.**
他去練習足球。

17 **She goes to swimming class.**
她去上游泳課。

18 **He goes to taekwondo class.**
他去上跆拳道課。

19 **Jane goes to dance class.**
珍去上舞蹈課。

國家圖書館出版品預行編目資料

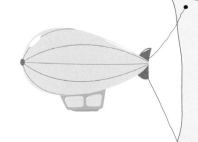

Fun 學美國各學科 Preschool 閱讀課本．5，初學單字篇 / Michael A. Putlack, e-Creative Contents 著 ； 歐寶妮譯．-- 二版．--［臺北市］：寂天文化，2018.12
　面；　公分

ISBN 978-986-318-448-5（平裝附光碟片）

1. 英語 2. 詞彙
805.12　　　　　　　　　　　　　　　　107020785

FÜN學 美國各學科
Preschool 閱讀課本 5 初學單字篇 二版

作　　者	Michael A. Putlack & e-Creative Contents
譯　　者	歐寶妮
編　　輯	賴祖兒／歐寶妮
主　　編	丁宥暄
內文排版	洪伊珊
封面設計	林書玉
製程管理	洪巧玲
出 版 者	寂天文化事業股份有限公司
電　　話	02-2365-9739
傳　　真	02-2365-9835
網　　址	www.icosmos.com.tw
讀者服務	onlineservice@icosmos.com.tw
出版日期	2018 年 12 月 二版一刷　080201

Copyright © 2018 by Key Publications
Photos Credits © Shutterstock Inc.
Copyright © 2018 by Cosmos Culture Ltd.
All rights reserved.

郵撥帳號　1998620-0　寂天文化事業股份有限公司
劃撥金額 600（含）元以上者，郵資免費。
訂購金額 600 元以下者，加收 65 元運費。
〔若有破損，請寄回更換，謝謝〕

FUN學美國各學科

Preschool 閱讀課本 _{二版}

二版

AMERiCAN SCHOOL TEXTBOOK

Reading Key

5

Preschool
初學單字篇

WORKBOOK
練習本

Workbook

Colors ①

A Read and write.

1. red

red

2. blue

blue

3. yellow

yellow

4. green

green

B Match and write.

1. a red hen

a red hen

2. a yellow chick

a yellow chick

3. a blue bird

a blue bird

4. a green tree

a green tree

4

C Circle the correct word for each sentence.

1.

It is a (**red**, **green**) car.

2.

It is a (**yellow**, **blue**) bus.

3.

It is a (**red**, **green**) taxi.

4.

It is a (**blue**, **green**) bicycle.

D Choose and write.

bicycle	bird	hen	chick

1.

What is it?
It is a yellow __**chick**__ .

2.

What is it?
It is a blue _____ .

3.

What is it?
It is a green _____ .

4.

What is it?
It is a red _____ .

2 Colors 2

A Read and write.

1.  orange
orange

2.  brown
brown

3.  black
black

4.  white
white

B Match and write.

1. an orange carrot   an orange carrot

2. a brown bear   a brown bear

3. a black cat   a black cat

4. a white dog   a white dog

5. a black and white penguin
a black and white penguin

Circle the correct word for each sentence.

1.

It is a (**white**, **black**) cat.

2.

It is a (**brown**, **white**) bear.

3.

It is a (**black**, **white**) dog.

4.

It is an (**orange**, **yellow**) carrot.

D **Circle the correct word for each sentence.**

1.

What am I?
⇨ I am black and white.
I am a (**penguin**, **bird**).

2.

What am I?
⇨ I am big and brown.
I am a (**penguin**, **bear**).

3.

What am I?
⇨ I am little and white.
I am a (**cat**, **dog**).

4.

What am I?
⇨ I am little and black.
I am a (**cat**, **dog**).

Shapes ①

A Read and write.

1. circle

circle

2. square

square

3.  triangle

triangle

4. rectangle

rectangle

B Match and write.

1. a red ball   a red ball ·

2. a brown chocolate   a brown chocolate ·

3. a green board   a green board ·

4. a yellow rectangle a yellow rectangle ·

5. two pyramids   two pyramids ·

6. two triangles   two triangles ·

Circle the correct word for each sentence.

1. It is a red (**circle**, **triangle**).

2. It is a blue (**square**, **rectangle**).

3. There are two (**circles, triangles**).

4. There are two (**squares, rectangles**).

D **Choose and write.**

| circle | squares | triangles | rectangles |

1. What do you see?
   I see one black __circle__ .

2. What do you see?
   I see two orange _____.

3. What do you see?
   I see two green _____.

4. What do you see?
   I see two blue _____.

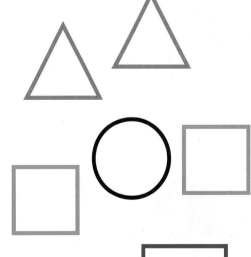

Shapes ②

A Read and write.

1.  diamond

diamond

2.  star

star

3.  oval

oval

4.  heart

heart

B Match and write.

1. road sign   road sign

2. egg   egg

3. gift box   gift box

4. cookie   cookie

5. a heart shape   a heart shape

1.

It is a (**diamond**, **heart**) shape.

2.

It is an (**oval, circle**) shape.

3.

It is a (**heart, oval**) shape.

4.

It is a (**heart, star**) shape.

D Choose and write.

gift box	star	oval	road sign

1.

What is it?
⇨It is an egg.
It is an __oval__ shape.

2.

What is it?
⇨It is a _____.
It is a heart shape.

3.

What is it?
⇨It is a _____.
It is a diamond shape.

4.

What is it?
⇨It is a cookie.
It is a _____ shape.

11

My Family

A Read and write.

1.  grandmother

   grandmother

2.  grandfather

   grandfather

3.  mother

   mother

4.  father

   father

B Match and write.

1. younger sister   younger sister •

2. older brother   older brother •

3. watch TV   watch TV •

4. cook   cook •

5. read a book   read a book •

6. sing a song   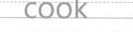sing a song •

C Circle the correct word for each sentence.

1. Who is this?
   This is my older (**sister**, **brother**).

2. Who is this?
   This is my younger (**sister, brother**).

3. Who is this?
   This is my (**grandmother, grandfather**).

4. Who is this?
   This is my (**grandmother, grandfather**).

D Choose and write.

| watching TV   reading a book   cooking   singing a song |

1.

What is Dad doing?
He is __**watching TV**__.

2.

What is Mom doing?
She is _____.

3.

What is my brother doing?
He is _____.

4.

What is your sister doing?
She is _____.

6 At School

A Read and write.

1.  teacher

   teacher

2.  student

   student

3.  classroom

   classroom

4.  playground

   playground

B Match and write.

1. library   library

2. cafeteria   cafeteria

3. reading   reading

4. writing   writing

5. painting   painting

6. playing   playing

1.

The girl is (**reading**, **writing**).

2.

The teacher is (**reading**, **writing**).

3.

Ann is (**playing**, **painting**).

4.

Ben is (**playing**, **painting**).

D Choose and write.

| cafeteria | library | board | classroom | playground |

1. The girl is reading in the __library__ .

2. The boy is playing on the _____ .

3. The teacher is writing on the _____ .

4. Ann is eating lunch in the _____ .

5. Ben is painting in the _____ .

7 After School ①

A Read and write.

1. cycling

   cycling

2.  jogging

   jogging

3.  roller-skating

   roller-skating

4.  swimming

   swimming

B Match and write.

1. ice skating   _ice skating_

2. sledding   _sledding_

3. playing soccer   _playing soccer_

4. playing baseball   _playing baseball_

5. playing basketball   _playing basketball_

6. playing volleyball   _playing volleyball_

Circle the correct word for each sentence.

1. They are (**swimming**, **skiing**).

2. They are (**snowboarding**, **sledding**).

3. They are playing (**basketball**, **volleyball**).

4. They are (**jogging**, **roller-skating**).

D **Choose and write.**

| roller-skating | ice skating | sledding | playing baseball |

1.

What is the boy doing?
He is ___ice skating___ .

2.

What is the girl doing?
She is _____ .

3.

What are the boys doing?
They are _____ .

4.

What are the girls doing?
They're _____ .

After School ②

A Read and write.

1. art class

art class

2. English class

English class

3. math class

math class

4. piano class

piano class

B Match and write.

1. dance class

dance class

2. soccer practice

soccer practice

3. taekwondo class

taekwondo class

4. swimming class

swimming class

C Circle the correct words for each sentence.

1. He goes to (soccer practice, math class).

2. She goes to (**swimming class, art class**).

3. He goes to (**taekwondo class, soccer practice**).

4. She goes to (**dance class, piano class**).

D Choose and write.

dance class   English class   math class   swimming class

1. What do you do after school?

I go to _____**English class**_____.

2. What do you do after school?

I go to _____.

3. What does he do after school?

He goes to _____.

4. What does she do after school?

She goes to _____.

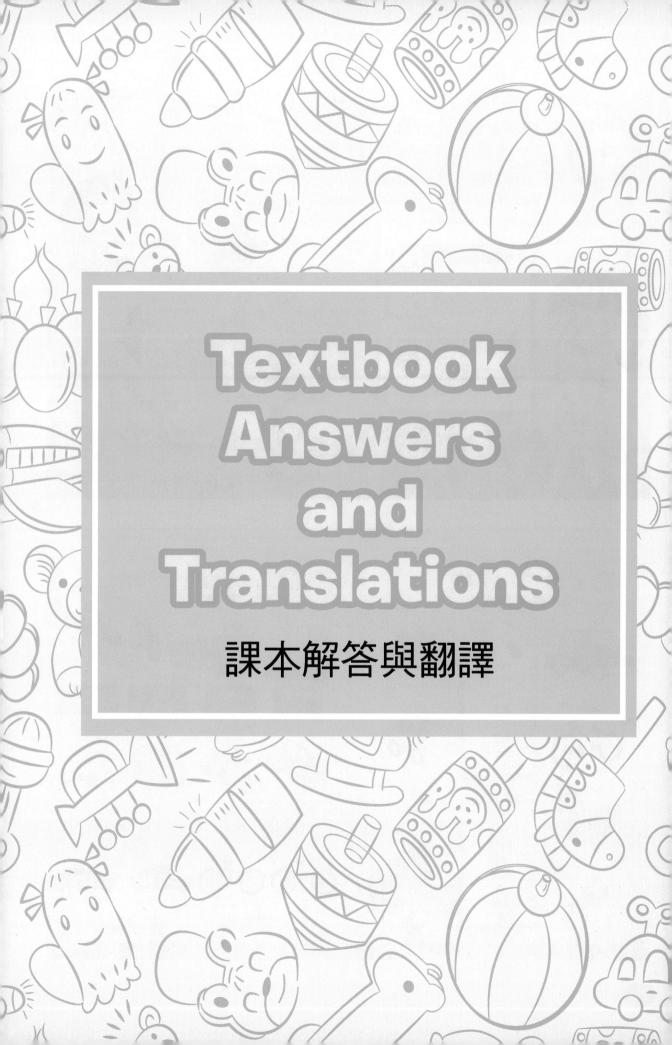

Textbook
Answers
and
Translations

課本解答與翻譯

UNIT 1 Colors 1 顏色 1

Key Words 關鍵字彙
閱讀以下單字。

red 紅色
yellow 黃色
blue 藍色
green 綠色

hen 母雞
chick 小雞
bird 鳥
tree 樹

6 7

Match Up 連連看
將圖片連接到正確的單字。

What Color? 什麼顏色？
在正確的圖片底下打勾。

red 紅色
blue 藍色
yellow 黃色
green 綠色

hen 母雞
chick 小雞
bird 鳥
tree 樹

a car 一台汽車
a bus 一台公車
a bicycle 一台腳踏車
a taxi 一台計程車

a red car 一台紅色的汽車
a yellow bus 一台黃色的公車
a blue bicycle 一台藍色的腳踏車
a green taxi 一台綠色的計程車

8 9

Colors 2 顏色 2

Key Words 關鍵字彙
閱讀以下單字。

orange 橘黃色

brown 棕色

black 黑色

white 白色

black and white 黑白相間

cat 貓

dog 狗

bear 熊

penguin 企鵝

14

15

Match Up 連連看
將單字連到正確的圖片。

orange 橘黃色

brown 棕色

black 黑色

white 白色

black and white 黑白相間

What Color? 什麼顏色？
在正確的圖片底下打勾。

a carrot 一根胡蘿蔔

a bear 一隻熊

a cat 一隻貓

a dog 一隻狗

a penguin 一隻企鵝

an orange carrot 一根橘黃色的胡蘿蔔

a brown bear 一隻棕色的熊

a black cat 一隻黑色的貓

a white dog 一隻白色的狗

a black and white penguin 一隻黑白相間的企鵝

16

17

24

What Is It? 牠是什麼？
圈出每個句子中正確的單字。

It is a (cat, dog).
牠是一隻（貓；狗）。

It is a (cat, dog).
牠是一隻（貓；狗）。

It is a (bear, bird).
牠是一隻（熊；鳥）。

It is a (penguin, bear).
牠是一隻（企鵝；熊）。

It is a (carrot, cat).
它是一根（胡蘿蔔；貓）。

牠是什麼顏色？
What Color Is It?
圈出每個句子中正確的單字。

It is white. 牠是白色的。
It is a (white, black) cat.
牠是一隻（白色的；黑色的）貓。

It is black. 牠是黑色的。
It is a (white, black) dog.
牠是隻（白色的；黑色的）狗。

It is brown. 牠是棕色的。
It is a (brown, white) bear.
牠是隻（棕色的；白色的）熊。

It is black and white.
It is a (black and white,
black and brown) penguin.
牠是黑白相間的。
牠是隻（黑白相間的；
黑棕相間的）的企鵝。

It is orange. 它是橘黃色的。
It is an (orange, yellow) carrot.
它是根（橘黃色的；黃色的）胡蘿蔔。

18　　19

I Can Read 我會閱讀
閱讀故事，將句子連到正確的圖片。

What Am I?
我是什麼？

I am big.
I am brown.
What am I?

我很大。
我是棕色的。
我是什麼呢？

I am little.
I am white.
What am I?

我很小。
我是白色的。
我是什麼呢？

I am big.
I am black and white.
What am I?

我很大。
我是黑白相間的。
我是什麼呢？

I am little.
I am black.
What am I?

我很小。
我是黑色的。
我是什麼呢？

20　　21

25

UNIT 3

Shapes ① 形狀 ①

Key Words 關鍵字彙
閱讀以下單字。

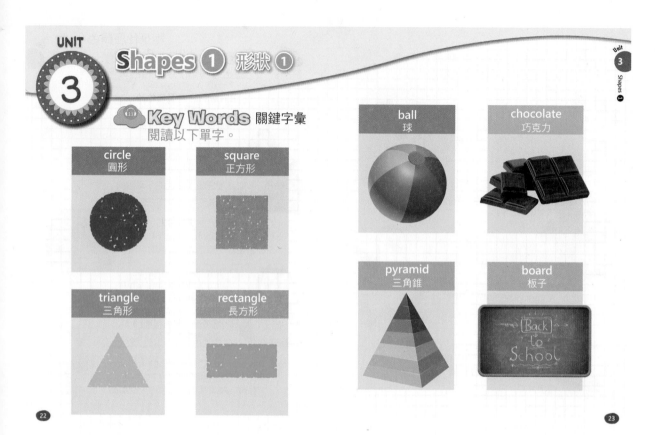

circle 圓形

square 正方形

triangle 三角形

rectangle 長方形

ball 球

chocolate 巧克力

pyramid 三角錐

board 板子

22

23

Match Up 連連看
將單字連到正確的圖片。

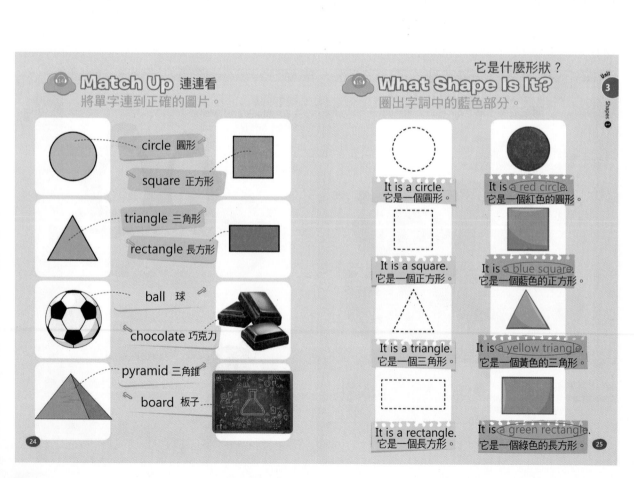

circle 圓形

square 正方形

triangle 三角形

rectangle 長方形

ball 球

chocolate 巧克力

pyramid 三角錐

board 板子

24

What Shape Is It?
它是什麼形狀？
圈出字詞中的藍色部分。

It is a circle.
它是一個圓形。

It is a red circle.
它是一個紅色的圓形。

It is a square.
它是一個正方形。

It is a blue square.
它是一個藍色的正方形。

It is a triangle.
它是一個三角形。

It is a yellow triangle.
它是一個黃色的三角形。

It is a rectangle.
它是一個長方形。

It is a green rectangle.
它是一個綠色的長方形。

25

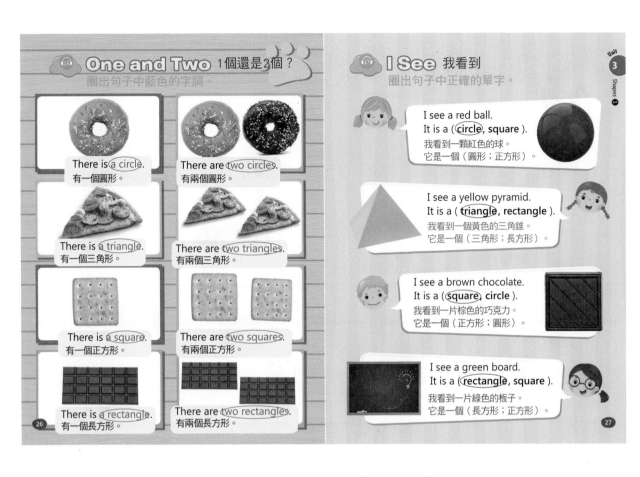

One and Two 1個還是2個？
圈出句子中藍色的字詞。

There is a circle.
有一個圓形。

There are two circles.
有兩個圓形。

There is a triangle.
有一個三角形。

There are two triangles.
有兩個三角形。

There is a square.
有一個正方形。

There are two squares.
有兩個正方形。

There is a rectangle.
有一個長方形。

There are two rectangles.
有兩個長方形。

I See 我看到
圈出句子中正確的單字。

I see a red ball.
It is a (circle, square).
我看到一顆紅色的球。
它是一個（圓形；正方形）。

I see a yellow pyramid.
It is a (triangle, rectangle).
我看到一個黃色的三角錐。
它是一個（三角形；長方形）。

I see a brown chocolate.
It is a (square, circle).
我看到一片棕色的巧克力。
它是一個（正方形；圓形）。

I see a green board.
It is a (rectangle, square).
我看到一片綠色的板子。
它是一個（長方形；正方形）。

26 · 27

I Can Read 我會閱讀
閱讀故事，並圈出正確的字詞。

What Do You See?
你看見什麼？

What do you see?
I see one yellow (triangle, circle).
你看見什麼？
我看見一個黃色的（三角形；圓形）。

What do you see?
I see two blue (squares, rectangles).
你看見什麼？
我看見兩個藍色的（正方形；長方形）。

What do you see?
I see two red (circles, triangles).
你看見什麼？
我看見兩個紅色的（圓形；三角形）。

What do you see?
I see two green (rectangles, squares).
你看見什麼？
我看見兩個綠色的（長方形；正方形）。

28 · 29

Shapes ② 形狀 ②

🔊19 Key Words 關鍵字彙
閱讀以下單字。

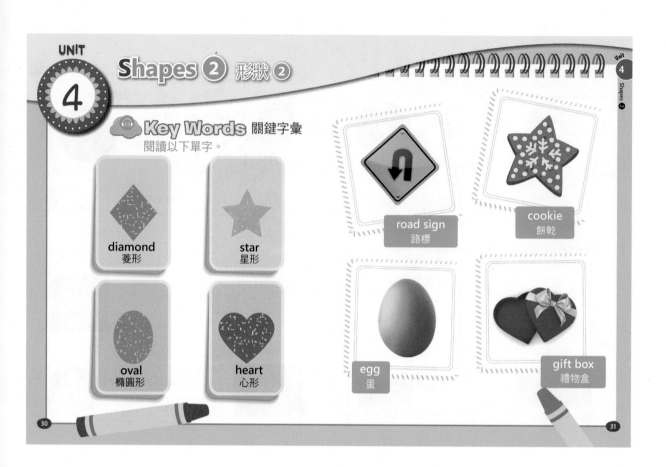

diamond 菱形

star 星形

oval 橢圓形

heart 心形

road sign 路標

cookie 餅乾

egg 蛋

gift box 禮物盒

30

31

🔊20 Match Up 連連看
將單字連到正確的圖片。

🔊21 What Shape Is It? 它是什麼形狀？
圈出藍色部分的字詞。

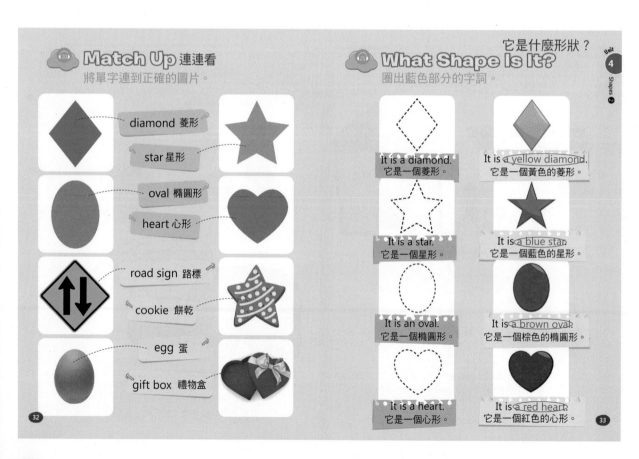

diamond 菱形

star 星形

oval 橢圓形

heart 心形

road sign 路標

cookie 餅乾

egg 蛋

gift box 禮物盒

It is a diamond.
它是一個菱形。

It is a yellow diamond.
它是一個黃色的菱形。

It is a star.
它是一個星形。

It is a blue star.
它是一個藍色的星形。

It is an oval.
它是一個橢圓形。

It is a brown oval.
它是一個棕色的橢圓形。

It is a heart.
它是一個心形。

It is a red heart.
它是一個紅色的心形。

32

33

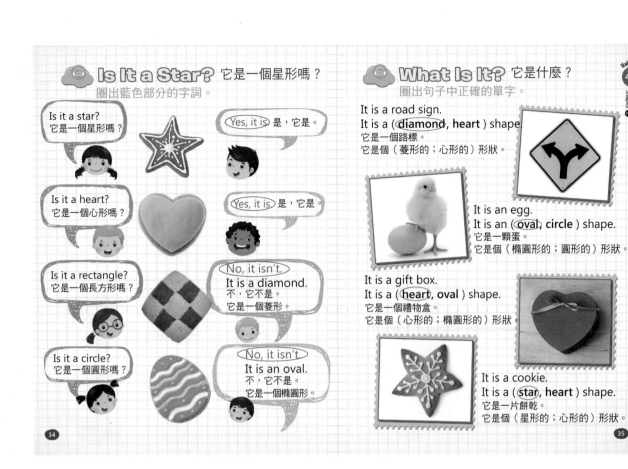

Is It a Star? 它是一個星形嗎？
圈出藍色部分的字詞。

Is it a star?
它是一個星形嗎？

Yes, it is 是，它是。

Is it a heart?
它是一個心形嗎？

Yes, it is 是，它是。

Is it a rectangle?
它是一個長方形嗎？

No, it isn't.
It is a diamond.
不，它不是。
它是一個菱形。

Is it a circle?
它是一個圓形嗎？

No, it isn't.
It is an oval.
不，它不是。
它是一個橢圓形。

34

What Is It? 它是什麼？
圈出句子中正確的單字。

It is a road sign.
It is a (diamond, heart) shape.
它是一個路標。
它是個（菱形的；心形的）形狀。

It is an egg.
It is an (oval, circle) shape.
它是一顆蛋。
它是個（橢圓形的；圓形的）形狀。

It is a gift box.
It is a (heart, oval) shape.
它是一個禮物盒。
它是個（心形的；橢圓形的）形狀。

It is a cookie.
It is a (star, heart) shape.
它是一片餅乾。
它是個（星形的；心形的）形狀。

35

I Can Read 我會閱讀
閱讀故事，圈出藍色部分
的字詞。

What Can You See?
你可以看見什麼？

I can see many stars.
They are blue and white.
我可以看見很多星形。
它們是藍色和白色的。

I can see many hearts.
They are red.
我可以看見很多心形。
它們是紅色的。

I can see many diamonds.
They are white
我可以看見很多鑽石。
它們是白色的。

I can see many eggs.
They are oval shapes.
我可以看見很多蛋。
它們是橢圓形。

36

37

29

Review Test 1

A Choose and write. 選出正確的字詞並填入空格。

square circle rectangle triangle brown orange black and white

1. a red <u>circle</u>
一個紅色的圓形

2. a blue <u>square</u>
一個藍色的正方形

3. a yellow <u>triangle</u>
一個黃色的三角形

4. a green <u>rectangle</u>
一個綠色的長方形

5. an <u>orange</u> carrot
一根橘黃色的胡蘿蔔

6. a <u>brown</u> bear
一隻棕色的熊

7. a <u>black and white</u> penguin
一隻黑白相間的企鵝

B Circle the correct answer for each sentence. 圈出正確的字詞。

1. I see a red (**hen**, chick).
我看見一隻紅色的（母雞；小雞）。

2. I see a yellow (**pyramid**, chocolate).
我看見一個黃色的（三角錐；巧克力）。

3. I see a green (ball, **board**).
我看見一塊綠色的（球；板子）。

4. I see an (**oval**, diamond) egg.
我看見一顆（橢圓形的；菱形的）蛋。

圈出每句中正確的字詞。
C Circle the correct answer for each sentence.

1. Is it a circle? 它是圓形嗎？
No, it isn't. It is an (**oval**, star).
不，它不是。它是個（橢圓形；星形）。

2. Is it a rectangle? 它是長方形嗎？
No, it isn't. It is a (circle, **triangle**).
不，它不是。它是個（圓形；三角形）。

3. Is it a heart shape? 它是心形的形狀嗎？
No, it isn't. It is a (diamond, **star**) shape.
不，它不是。它是個（菱形的；星形的）形狀。

4. Is it a diamond shape? 它是菱形的形狀嗎？
No, it isn't. It is a (**heart**, oval) shape.
不，它不是。它是個（心形的；橢圓形的）形狀。

D Match the sentences with the pictures.
將句子連接到正確的圖片。

1. It is a chick. 牠是隻小雞。
It is a yellow chick.
牠是隻黃色的小雞。

2. It is a chocolate.
它是片巧克力。
It is a brown chocolate.
它是片棕色的巧克力。

3. It is a gift box. 它是禮物盒。
It is a heart shape.
它是心形的形狀。

4. It is a road sign.它是路標。
It is a diamond shape.
它是菱形的形狀。

38   39

UNIT 5

My Family 我的家人

Key Words 關鍵字彙
閱讀以下單字。

grandmother 奶奶
grandma 奶奶
grandfather 爺爺
grandpa 爺爺
older brother 哥哥
sister 姐姐
brother 弟弟
mother 母親
mom 媽媽
father 父親
dad 爸爸
younger sister 妹妹

40   41

Match Up 連連看
將字詞連接到正確的圖片。

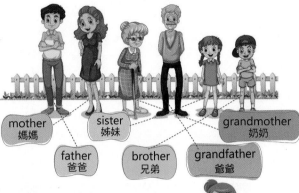

mother 媽媽

sister 姊妹

grandmother 奶奶

father 爸爸

brother 兄弟

grandfather 爺爺

watch TV 看電視

cook 做菜

read a book 閱讀書籍

sing a song 唱歌

42

 Who Is This? 這是誰？
圈出每句中正確的單字。

This is my (mother, father).
這是我的（媽媽；爸爸）。

This is my (mother, father).
這是我的（媽媽；爸爸）。

This is my (sister, brother).
這是我的（姊妹；兄弟）。

This is my (sister, brother).
這是我的（姊妹；兄弟）。

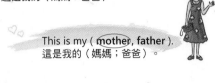
This is my (grandmother, grandfather).
這是我的（奶奶；爺爺）。

This is my (grandmother, grandfather).
這是我的（奶奶；爺爺）。

43

這是你的姊妹嗎？

 Is This Your Sister?
圈出字詞 Yes 和 is，在字詞 No 和 isn't 底下劃線。

Is this your sister?
這是你的姐妹嗎？
Yes, it is. 是的，她是。
She is my younger sister.
她是我的妹妹。

Is this your brother?
這是你的兄弟嗎？
Yes, it is. 是的，他是。
He is my older brother.
他是我的哥哥。

Is this your father?
這是你的爸爸嗎？
No, it isn't. 不，他不是。
He is my grandfather.
他是我的爺爺。

44

Is this your mother?
這是你的媽媽嗎？
No, it isn't. 不，她不是。
She is my grandmother.
她是我的奶奶。

她正在做什麼？

What Is She Doing?
圈出字詞中有 ing的部分。

My mom is cooking.
我媽正在做菜。

My dad is watching TV.
我爸正在看電視。

My sister is reading a book.
我妹妹正在看書。

My brother is singing a song.
我哥哥正在唱歌。

My grandpa is reading a newspaper.
我爺爺正在閱讀報紙。

45

31

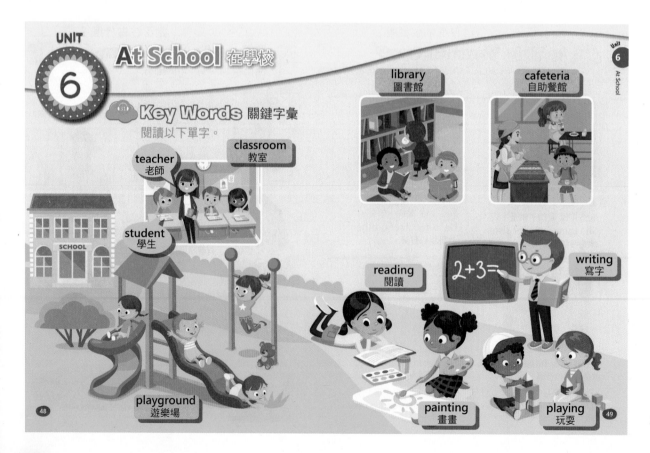

Match Up 連連看
將單字連接到正確的圖片。

teacher
老師

student
學生

classroom
教室

playground
遊樂場

library
圖書館

cafeteria
自助餐館

50

What Is He Doing? 他正在做什麼？
圈出每個句子中正確的單字。

The boy is (reading, writing).
那個男孩（正在閱讀；正在寫字）。

The girl is (playing, painting).
那個女孩（正在玩耍；正在畫畫）。

The teacher is (reading, writing).
那位老師（正在閱讀；正在寫字）。

Ben is (playing, painting).
班（正在玩耍；正在畫畫）。

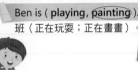

Ann is (eating, eat) lunch.
安（正在吃；吃）午餐。

51

Is She Doing? 她正在？
圈出字詞 Yes 和 is，在字詞 No 和 isn't 底下劃線。

Is the girl reading a book?
那個女孩正在閱讀書籍嗎？
Yes, she is. 對，她正在閱讀書籍。

Is the boy playing?
那個男孩正在玩耍嗎？
Yes, he is.
對，他正在玩耍。

Is the teacher singing?
那個老師正在唱歌嗎？
No, she isn't. She is writing.
不，不是。她正在寫字。

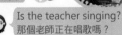
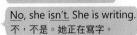

Is the student writing?
那個學生正在寫字嗎？
No, he isn't. He is painting.
不，不是。他正在畫畫。

52

Where Is She? 她在哪裡？
圈出每個句子中正確的單字。

The girl is reading in the (library, playground).
那個女孩正在（圖書館；操場）閱讀。

The boy is playing on the (library, playground).
那個男孩正在（圖書館；操場）玩耍。

Ben is painting in the (classroom, cafeteria).
班正在（教室；自助餐館）畫畫。

Ann is eating lunch in the (classroom, cafeteria).
安正在（教室；自助餐館）吃午餐。

The teacher is writing on the (board, table).
那個老師正在（板子上；桌上）寫字。

53

33

I Can Read 我會閱讀

閱讀故事，並圈出句子中藍色的字詞。

This is Jane. 這是珍。
She is painting in the classroom.
她正在教室裡畫畫。

This is Mike. 這是麥可。
He is playing on the playground.
他正在遊樂場裡玩耍。

This is Ben. 這是班。
He is reading a book in the library.
他正在圖書館裡閱讀書籍。

This is Ann. 這是安。
She is writing on the board.
她正在板子上寫字。

54

55

UNIT 7

After school ❶
放學後 ❶

Key Words 關鍵字彙
閱讀以下字詞。

cycling 騎腳踏車

jogging 慢跑

roller-skating 溜直排輪

swimming 游泳

ice skating 溜冰

skiing 滑雪

snowboarding 單板滑雪

sledding 乘雪橇

playing soccer 踢足球

playing baseball 打棒球

playing basketball 打籃球

playing volleyball 打排球

56

57

Match Up 連連看

將單字連接到正確的圖片。

cycling
騎腳踏車

jogging
慢跑

roller-skating
溜直排輪

swimming
游泳

ice skating
溜冰

skiing
滑雪

snowboarding
單板滑雪

sledding
乘雪橇

58

What Are They Doing?

圈出句子中正確的字詞。

They are (jogging, cycling).
他們（正在慢跑；正在騎腳踏車）。

They are (roller-skating, ice skating).
他們（正在溜直排輪；正在溜冰）。

They are (cycling, sledding).
他們（正在騎腳踏車；正在乘雪橇）。

They are (swimming, skiing).
他們（正在游泳；正在滑雪）。

59

Are They Doing? 他們正在？

圈出字詞 Yes 和 is，在字詞 No 和 isn't 底下劃線。

Are they ice skating?
他們正在溜冰嗎？

Yes, they are.
對，他們正在溜冰。

Are they skiing?
他們正在滑雪嗎？

Yes, they are.
對，他們正在滑雪。

Are they snowboarding?
他們正在玩單板滑雪嗎？

No, they aren't.
They're sledding.
不，不是。
他們正在乘雪橇。

Are they sledding?
他們正在乘雪橇嗎？

No, they aren't. They're snowboarding.
不，不是。他們正在玩單板滑雪。

60

Are You Doing? 你正在？

在藍色字詞底下劃線。

Are you playing soccer?
你正在踢足球嗎？

Yes, I am.
對，沒錯。

Are you playing baseball?
你正在打棒球嗎？

Yes, I am.
對，沒錯。

Are you playing volleyball?
你正在打排球嗎？

No, I'm not. 不，不是。
I'm playing basketball.
我正在打籃球。

Are you playing basketball?
你正在打籃球嗎？

No, I'm not. 不，不是。
I'm playing volleyball.
我正在打排球。

61

I Can Read 我會閱讀
閱讀故事，圈出藍色部分的字詞。

What Are They Doing?
他們正在做什麼？

The boy is snowboarding.
那個男孩正在用滑雪板滑雪。

The girls are skiing.
女孩們正在滑雪。

The boys are sledding.
男孩們正在乘雪橇。

The boy is jogging in the park.
那個男孩正在公園裡慢跑。

The girl is roller-skating in the park.
那個女孩正在公園裡溜直排輪。

The boys are playing baseball in the park.
男孩們正在公園裡打棒球。

62

63

UNIT 8
After school ②
放學後 ②

Key Words 關鍵字彙
閱讀以下字詞。

art class 美術課

英文課 English class

Aa Bb Cc Dd Ee Ff Gg Hh Ii Jj Kk

math class 數學課

piano class 鋼琴課

dance class 舞蹈課

soccer practice 足球練習

taekwondo class 跆拳道課

swimming class 游泳課

64

65

Match Up 連連看
將單字連接到正確的圖片。

I Go to 我去
圈出藍色部分的字詞。

art class 美術課
English class 英文課
math class 數學課
piano class 鋼琴課
dance class 舞蹈課
soccer practice 足球練習
taekwondo class 跆拳道課
swimming class 游泳課

I go to English class. 我去上英文課。
I go to math class. 我去上數學課。
I go to piano class. 我去上鋼琴課。
I go to art class. 我去上美術課。
I go to dance class. 我去上舞蹈課。

66

67

He Goes to 他去
圈出藍色部分的字詞。

What Do You Do? 你做什麼？
圈出句子中正確的單字。

He goes to soccer practice. 他去練習足球。
She goes to swimming class. 她去上游泳課。
He goes to taekwondo class. 他去上跆拳道課。
Jane goes to dance class. 珍去上舞蹈課。
Ben goes to piano class. 班去上鋼琴課。

What do you do after school? 你放學後通常會做什麼？
I go to (math, English) class. 我去上（數學；英文）課。

What do you do after school? 你放學後通常會做什麼？
I go to (art, piano) class. 我去上（美術；鋼琴）課。

What do you do after school? 你放學後通常會做什麼？
I go to (art, piano) class. 我去上（美術；鋼琴）課。

What do you do after school? 你放學後通常會做什麼？
I go to (dance, swimming) class. 我去上（舞蹈；游泳）課。

68

69

37

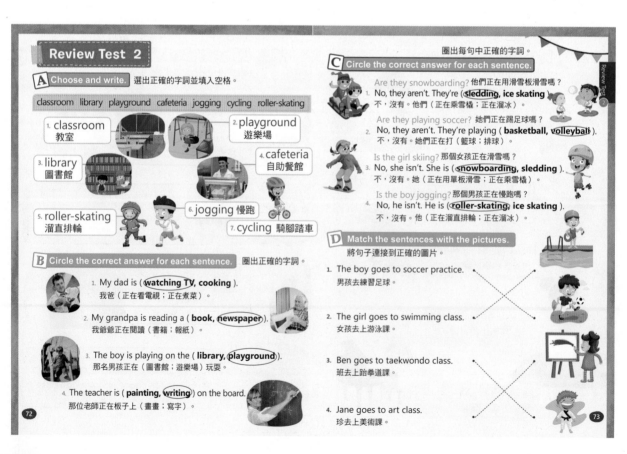

Daily Test
Answers
課堂練習解答

Colors 1

A Read and write.

1. red — red
2. blue — blue
3. yellow — yellow
4. green — green

B Match and write.

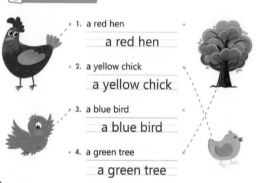

1. a red hen — a red hen
2. a yellow chick — a yellow chick
3. a blue bird — a blue bird
4. a green tree — a green tree

C Circle the correct word for each sentence.

1. It is a (**red**, green) car.
2. It is a (**yellow**, blue) bus.
3. It is a (red, **green**) taxi.
4. It is a (**blue**, green) bicycle.

D Choose and write.

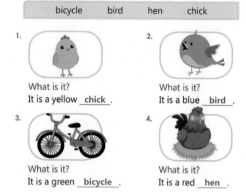

bicycle	bird	hen	chick

1. What is it?
It is a yellow **chick**.

2. What is it?
It is a blue **bird**.

3. What is it?
It is a green **bicycle**.

4. What is it?
It is a red **hen**.

4

5

Colors 2

A Read and write.

1. orange — orange
2. brown — brown
3. black — black
4. white — white

B Match and write.

1. an orange carrot — an orange carrot
2. a brown bear — a brown bear
3. a black cat — a black cat
4. a white dog — a white dog
5. a black and white penguin — a black and white penguin

C Circle the correct word for each sentence.

1. It is a (**white**, black) cat.
2. It is a (**brown**, white) bear.
3. It is a (**black**, white) dog.
4. It is an (**orange**, yellow) carrot.

D Circle the correct word for each sentence.

1. What am I?
⇨ I am black and white.
I am a (**penguin**, bird).

2. What am I?
⇨ I am big and brown.
I am a (penguin, **bear**).

3. What am I?
⇨ I am little and white.
I am a (cat, **dog**).

4. What am I?
⇨ I am little and black.
I am a (**cat**, dog).

6

7

40

3 Shapes ①

A Read and write.

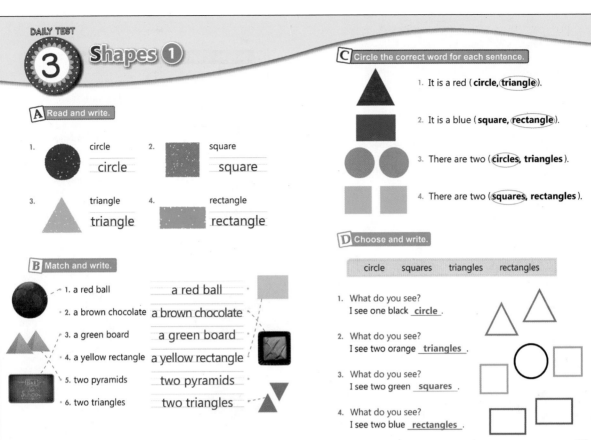

1. circle — circle
2. square — square
3. triangle — triangle
4. rectangle — rectangle

B Match and write.

1. a red ball — a red ball
2. a brown chocolate — a brown chocolate
3. a green board — a green board
4. a yellow rectangle — a yellow rectangle
5. two pyramids — two pyramids
6. two triangles — two triangles

C Circle the correct word for each sentence.

1. It is a red (circle, **triangle**).
2. It is a blue (square, **rectangle**).
3. There are two (**circles**, triangles).
4. There are two (**squares**, rectangles).

D Choose and write.

| circle | squares | triangles | rectangles |

1. What do you see?
   I see one black **circle**.
2. What do you see?
   I see two orange **triangles**.
3. What do you see?
   I see two green **squares**.
4. What do you see?
   I see two blue **rectangles**.

8

9

4 Shapes ②

A Read and write.

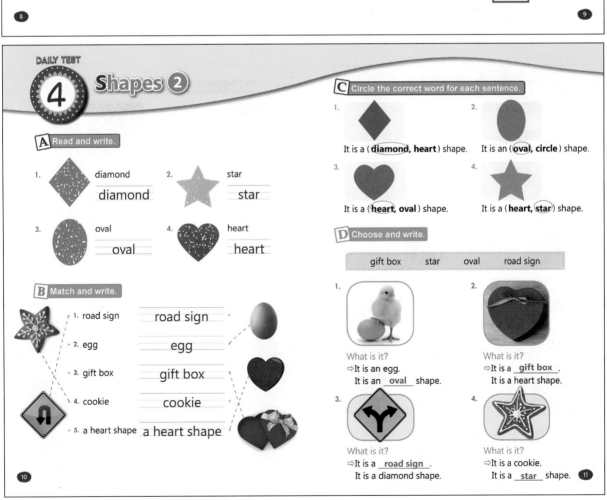

1. diamond — diamond
2. star — star
3. oval — oval
4. heart — heart

B Match and write.

1. road sign — road sign
2. egg — egg
3. gift box — gift box
4. cookie — cookie
5. a heart shape — a heart shape

C Circle the correct word for each sentence.

1. It is a (**diamond**, heart) shape.
2. It is an (**oval**, circle) shape.
3. It is a (**heart**, oval) shape.
4. It is a (heart, **star**) shape.

D Choose and write.

| gift box | star | oval | road sign |

1. What is it?
   ⇨ It is an egg.
   It is an **oval** shape.
2. What is it?
   ⇨ It is a **gift box**.
   It is a heart shape.
3. What is it?
   ⇨ It is a **road sign**.
   It is a diamond shape.
4. What is it?
   ⇨ It is a cookie.
   It is a **star** shape.

10

11

41

5 My Family

A Read and write.

1. grandmother
grandmother

2. grandfather
grandfather

3. mother
mother

4. father
father

B Match and write.

1. younger sister   younger sister
2. older brother   older brother
3. watch TV   watch TV
4. cook   cook
5. read a book   read a book
6. sing a song   sing a song

C Circle the correct word for each sentence.

1. Who is this?
This is my older (**sister**, **brother**).

2. Who is this?
This is my younger (**sister**, **brother**).

3. Who is this?
This is my (**grandmother**, **grandfather**).

4. Who is this?
This is my (**grandmother**, **grandfather**).

D Choose and write.

watching TV   reading a book   cooking   singing a song

1. What is Dad doing?
He is __watching TV__.

2. What is Mom doing?
She is __cooking__.

3. What is my brother doing?
He is __singing a song__.

4. What is your sister doing?
She is __reading a book__.

12   13

---

6 At School

A Read and write.

1. teacher
teacher

2. student
student

3. classroom
classroom

4. playground
playground

B Match and write.

1. library   library
2. cafeteria   cafeteria
3. reading   reading
4. writing   writing
5. painting   painting
6. playing   playing

C Circle the correct word for each sentence.

1. The girl is (**reading**, **writing**).

2. The teacher is (**reading**, **writing**).

3. Ann is (**playing**, **painting**).

4. Ben is (**playing**, **painting**).

D Choose and write.

cafeteria   library   board   classroom   playground

1. The girl is reading in the __library__.

2. The boy is playing on the __playground__.

3. The teacher is writing on the __board__.

4. Ann is eating lunch in the __cafeteria__.

5. Ben is painting in the __classroom__.

14   15

7 After School ❶

A Read and write.

1. cycling
cycling

2. jogging
jogging

3. roller-skating
roller-skating

4. swimming
swimming

B Match and write.

1. ice skating — ice skating
2. sledding — sledding
3. playing soccer — playing soccer
4. playing baseball — playing baseball
5. playing basketball — playing basketball
6. playing volleyball — playing volleyball

C Circle the correct word for each sentence.

1. They are (swimming, **skiing**).

2. They are (**snowboarding**, sledding).

3. They are playing (basketball, **volleyball**).

4. They are (**jogging**, roller-skating).

D Choose and write.

roller-skating   ice skating   sledding   playing baseball

1.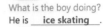
What is the boy doing?
He is ___ice skating___ .

2.
What is the girl doing?
She is ___roller-skating___ .

3.
What are the boys doing?
They are ___playing baseball___ .

4.
What are the girls doing?
They're ___sledding___ .

16   17

8 After School ❷

A Read and write.

1. art class
art class

2. English class
English class

3. math class
math class

4. piano class
piano class

B Match and write.

1. dance class
dance class

2. soccer practice
soccer practice

3. taekwondo class
taekwondo class

4. swimming class
swimming class

C Circle the correct words for each sentence.

1. He goes to (**soccer practice**, math class).

2. She goes to (swimming class, **art class**).

3. He goes to (**taekwondo class**, soccer practice).

4. She goes to (dance class, **piano class**).

D Choose and write.

dance class   English class   math class   swimming class

1. What do you do after school?
I go to ___English class___ .

2. What do you do after school?
I go to ___math class___ .

3. What does he do after school?
He goes to ___swimming class___ .

4. What does she do after school?
She goes to ___dance class___ .

18   19

43